Bunbun
at the Fair

Sharon Pierce McCullough

Barefoot Books
Celebrating Art and Story

Bunbun, Benny and Bibi are off to the fair.

There are lots of things for them to see and do.

Bunbun sees a funny clown.

The clown teaches him to juggle.

Benny and Bibi
ride the motorcars.

Benny and Bunbun play ring toss.

Bibi wins a prize.

Where is Bunbun?

Benny and
Bibi can't find
him anywhere.

Bibi checks the merry-go-round.

No Bunbun!

Benny looks in the petting zoo.

Pony Rides

No Bunbun!

There's Bunbun!

One more ride for Benny, Bunbun and Bibi,

until
Bunbun's
next fair.

For Randy,
my "fun and games" boy

Barefoot Books
3 Bow Street, 3rd Floor
Cambridge, MA 02138

This book is printed on 100% acid-free paper
The illustrations were prepared in
Prisma color pencils on Bristol Board
Design by Jennie Hoare, England
Typeset in 58pt Providence-Sans Bold
Color separation by Bright Arts, Singapore
Printed and bound in Hong Kong by
South China Printing Co. (1988) Ltd.

U.S. Cataloging-in-Publication Data
   (Library of Congress Standards)

McCullough, Sharon Pierce.
 Bunbun at the fair / Sharon Pierce McCullough.
   p. cm.
Summary: While Bunbun is enjoying all of the activities of his first
fair, he gets separated from his brother and sister.
  ISBN 1-84148-900-X
  [1. Fairs--Fiction. 2. Lost children--Fiction. 3. Brothers and
sisters--Fiction. 4. Rabbits--Fiction.] I. Title.
  PZ7.M47841496 Bu 2002
  [E]--dc21

                              2001005067

1 3 5 7 9 8 6 4 2

Barefoot Books
Celebrating Art and Story

At Barefoot Books, we celebrate art and story with books that open the hearts and minds of children from all walks of life, inspiring them to read deeper, search further, and explore their own creative gifts. Taking our inspiration from many different cultures, we focus on themes that encourage independence of spirit, enthusiasm for learning, and acceptance of other traditions. Thoughtfully prepared by writers, artists, and storytellers from all over the world, our products combine the best of the present with the best of the past to educate our children as the caretakers of tomorrow.

www.barefootbooks.com